A Teacher's Promise

To an extra-special teacher, Jane Skovholt, who dedicated her
professional career and her endless passion to teaching and
caring for those who needed it the very most.

And to Mary Bresadola, a woman who has taught all who know
her how to live each day with gratitude, grace, and courage.

—*Rachel*

To David, Skyler, and Griffin.
Thanks for making me laugh.

—*Priscilla*

Published by Redleaf Lane
An imprint of Redleaf Press
10 Yorkton Court
Saint Paul, MN 55117
www.RedleafLane.org

Text © 2016 by Rachel Robertson
Illustration © 2016 by Priscilla Prentice

First edition 2016
Book jacket and interior design by Jim Handrigan
Main body text set in Abril Text

U17-06

A Teacher's
PROMISE

Written by
Rachel Robertson

Illustrated by
Priscilla Prentice

Redleaf
Lane

In every classroom
one person is there
to show you the way with kindness and care.

A person who wants to know all about you—
the things that you like,
the things that you do.

I bet you don't know
who that person could be.

That person's
your teacher.
That person is me!

My job is to teach you and help you to grow,
To show you new things to learn and to know.

I'll help you discover. I'll help you explore.
We'll learn all you want to—and then we'll learn more!

We'll find what you're good at
And what you like best.
We'll try new ideas, put them all to the test.

We'll dream great big dreams
And we'll think great big thoughts.
We'll wonder and ponder and marvel a lot.

Maybe it's math, or it's science, or art.
We'll find out together the ways you are smart!

We'll do it your own way. Your way is what's best.
It's how you get ready for all of the rest.

You won't have to win any knowing-stuff races.
I'll make sure you learn at your very own paces!

And if there's a time you don't know what to do,
I'll give you a boost, or a nudge, or a clue.

And hey, while we're at it,
we'll build more than smarts.
We'll pay close attention
to what's in your hearts.

Silly

We'll talk about feelings
and what you can do
when you're feeling ecstatic,
or silly, or blue.

We'll learn about friendships and make a few too.
We'll strive to be kind as we do what we do.

We'll aim to be patient and try hard to share.
We'll think before doing and use words with care.

I'll believe you can do it, yep, no matter what:
When you're feeling just great or you're stuck in a rut.

I'll never run out of high fives, winks, or hugs.
Whenever you need it, I'll squeeze you so snug.

I'll laugh at your jokes and I'll tell a few too.
We'll giggle, and chuckle, and snort hooty-hoo!

When you have a secret or story to tell,
I'll sit down and listen. I do that quite well.

We won't sit too long, though. We'll get up and go!
We'll move to stay healthy—from head down to toe.

We'll hop, skip, and run! We'll climb, swing, and sway!
We'll make zippity-zoom for our learning and play.

And there will be times when things don't go just right.
We'll make some mistakes, indeed, try as we might.

But mistakes are okay. Mistakes help us grow.
They help us to learn and to know what we know.

So no matter how well we're getting things done,
We'll grin ear to ear and have oodles of fun!

There's so much to do, and to be, and to see—
What an adventure for you and for me!

All this and more I promise we'll do.
Each day I'll be proud of the you that is you.

A Note from the Author

A really great teacher can influence a child for a lifetime.
That's pretty powerful stuff, isn't it?

I wrote this book to remind us all—teachers, families, and
policymakers—that the most effective teaching and the most
meaningful learning don't come from testing, or an unbalanced
emphasis on academics, or treating the earliest years as simply
a preparatory phase for later life. They come from every child
having a teacher who believes in her, who helps her discover
what she's good at, and who supports her in her efforts to
do what she enjoys doing[1]. When a teacher provides these
things, children are able to blossom and grow to their fullest
potential—and even enjoy learning!

I have been lucky enough to experience firsthand how a great
teacher can influence a child, thanks to the many remarkable
teachers who have influenced my life and my daughters' lives.
I believe all children deserve to hear the messages in this book
and to have teachers who can make these promises. And all
teachers who have committed their lives to children deserve the
time and respect they need to follow through on the promises
they make.

1. For more about this idea, check out Gallup's "The New Bill of Rights for All Students."